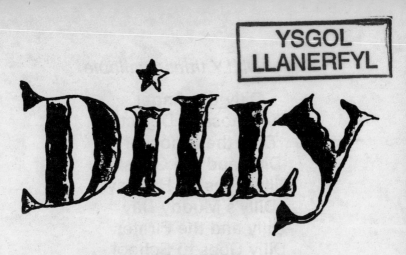

DiLLY

AND THE BIG KIDS

All this time Dilly had been standing there with a stupid look on his face. I don't think he could believe that Donnie, Delbert and Davy were actually in *his* house.

But they were, and they seemed to be enjoying themselves. They kept asking for more of Grandma's cakes, and they even laughed at Grandpa's dreadful jokes and stories.

"Ooh," said Dilly happily as he handed round another plate of cakes. "This is just like having a party, isn't it?"

Other DILLY titles available

Dilly the Angel
Dilly Dinosaur, Detective
Dilly the Dinosaur
Dilly and the Ghost
Dilly Goes on Holiday
Dilly's Muddy Day
Dilly and the Pirates
Dilly Goes to School
Dilly Dinosaur, Superstar
Dilly and His Swamp Lizard
Dilly Goes Swamp Wallowing
Dilly and the Tiger
Dilly Tells the Truth
Dilly and the Vampire

for younger readers

Dilly's Birthday Party

activity book

Dilly's Day Out

TONY BRADMAN

DiLLy

AND THE BIG KIDS

Illustrated by Susan Hellard

MAMMOTH

First published in Great Britain 1991
by Piccadilly Press Ltd
Published 1993 by Mammoth
an imprint of Reed International Books Ltd
Michelin House, 81 Fulham Road, London SW3 6RB
and Auckland, Melbourne, Singapore and Toronto

Reprinted 1994, 1995 (twice), 1996

Text copyright © Tony Bradman 1991
Illustrations copyright © Susan Hellard 1991

The right of Tony Bradman and Susan Hellard to be identified as
author and illustrator of this work has been asserted by them in
accordance with the Copyright, Designs and Patents Act 1988.

ISBN 0 7493 0735 6

A CIP catalogue record for this title
is available from the British Library

Printed and bound in Great Britain
by Cox & Wyman Ltd, Reading, Berkshire

Contents

DILLY TO THE RESCUE

The other day I was in my bedroom when I heard Mother calling me from downstairs.

"Dorla! Could you come here for a second, please?"

She was in the kitchen with my little brother, Dilly. He was standing on a chair, and Mother was draping an old green curtain over his shoulders. He was wearing a T-shirt with a big orange letter 'D' sewn on it.

"Mother's making me a Captain Dinosaur costume," said Dilly with a big smile. He was very excited. "Isn't it *terrific*?"

To tell the truth, I was sick to death of Dilly's favourite new cartoon character. Captain Dinosaur is a super-hero who flies around rescuing anyone who gets into trouble. I think he's boring, and Dilly goes on about him the whole time.

"Just hold this, will you, Dorla?" said Mother. I took one corner of the curtain from her while she pinned another part together. "There, that should do it. Umm, it's not bad, even though I say so myself."

Mother was right. I had to admit Dilly did look good in his costume. He spent the next couple of hours in his room, pretending to save some of his toys. And as usual, he sang the Captain Dinosaur theme song while he played.

"Brighter than the brightest star," it went. "Faster than a dino-car. See him fly, yes, see him soar! Got a problem? Send for . . .*Captain Dinosaur!*" He was still singing as he came down the stairs.

"Oh, Dilly," said Mother, laughing. I was giggling as well. "You're so funny sometimes!"

Dilly stopped in his tracks.

"This *isn't* funny, Mother," he said

with his I'm-Being-Very-Serious-Look on his face. "Now I've got my costume, *I'm* going to save anyone who's in trouble, too."

"Well, actually, Dilly," said Mother, "I know a little dinosaur who might need saving fairly soon. He'll probably get told off later if he doesn't tidy up the mess in his room."

Dilly looked confused for a moment. Then he realised Mother was talking about *him*, and his face fell.

"But Mother . . ." he said.

"No buts, Dilly. I want that room tidied," said Mother. Then she smiled again. "And just to make it easier, if you can get it done in the next ten minutes, I'll take you and Dorla to the park. Is it a deal?"

Dilly simply *adores* going to the park. So without even bothering to reply, he turned and dashed upstairs, his cape billowing behind him. He charged into his room, and shut the door with a . . . SLAM!

There was the sound of toys being kicked under the bed or thrown into cupboards. Mother winced, and when the crashing and smashing was finished, Dilly re-appeared downstairs.

"I've done it, Mother!" he said, breathlessly. Then he started bouncing up and down. "Can we go now? And can I keep my Captain Dinosaur costume on? Please? *Please*?"

"Oh no, I'm not going out with him dressed like *that*," I said. "Suppose we meet someone I know? It will be *so* embarrassing."

But Mother didn't agree. In fact, she said she thought he looked *sweet*. You know, grown-ups amaze me sometimes!

"Of course you can wear your costume, Dilly," she said. "But you'll have to behave. And stop jumping up and down, will you? It's very irritating."

Dilly did what he was told. Then he stuck his tongue out and gave me his I've-Got-My-Own-Way-So-There-You-Horrible-Meanie look. I took no notice.

I wish I could have said the same

about the dinosaurs at the park. They stared at us from the moment we went through the gate. Or rather, they stared and *smiled* at Dilly, much to my horror and his delight. He loves being the centre of attention.

On our way to the swings we had to walk past a giant swamp oak. A friend of Mother's was standing underneath it with her small daughter. We could see the little dinosaur was crying. Mother said hello, and asked what was wrong.

"Our pet lizard ran away," said Mother's friend. "It climbed this tree, and now I don't think it can get down."

We looked up, and sure enough, there was a lizard hanging on tightly to a branch. It was very still, and its eyes were big and round. Mother said that perhaps we ought to ask one of the park-keepers to do something.

"No need for that, ma'am," said someone behind us. "Stand back. This is a job for . . . *Captain Dinosaur*!"

We all turned – and were just in time to see Dilly making his first mistake. He scrambled up the trunk of the tree as fast as he could go. He was humming the Captain Dinosaur theme song, and his eyes were fixed on the pet lizard above.

"Dilly, come down from there this instant!" said Mother.

But Dilly wasn't listening. He reached the branch where the lizard was, then started crawling along it.

"Fear not, small creature!" he said in his Captain Dinosaur voice. "I'll soon have you safe and sound, back on the ground!"

And that's when Dilly made his second mistake.

He looked down.

It obviously hadn't occurred to him just how high the branch was. He suddenly went pale green with panic, gripped on grimly with all four paws *and* his tail and . . .

That's right, you guessed it, he let rip

with an ultra-special, 150-mile-per-hour super-scream, the kind that makes everyone in the park run over to see what's going on.

In fact, quite a crowd gathered under that tree. A crowd that happened to include *several* dinosaurs from my school. I wanted the marsh grass to open up and swallow me.

Dilly's scream had scared the pet lizard so much it had shot along the branch past him, and down the trunk of the tree. The little dinosaur was holding it, so at least she was happy now.

But Dilly wouldn't budge. He clung on to the branch with all his strength, his eyes screwed shut. He wouldn't even answer when Mother called out to him. By now she was really worried.

"How on earth is he going to get down?" she said.

"He could try flying," I said. "Isn't that what Captain Dinosaur does?"

Mother gave me a stern look, the one that means, "You're not really helping, Dorla," so I didn't say anything else.

There was no need for *me* to speak, in any case. It seemed as if every dinosaur in the crowd had a brilliant idea for rescuing Dilly. Unfortunately, none of them worked.

We tried telling him not to be afraid, and to edge slowly back the way he had come. A young dinosaur climbed up to give him a paw along the branch, which wasn't strong enough to support a grown-up. Dilly just held on more tightly.

The park-keeper even went to fetch a ladder, but it turned out to be too short. Mother went up it anyway, for one last try at talking him down.

Dilly opened an eye and looked at her . . . Then he closed it again, quickly. He wasn't going to move.

"He could be up there all night at this rate," said the park-keeper. Mother looked horrified. "We'll just have to send for the fire brigade."

The fire engine arrived with its siren whooping and its lights flashing. The crew jumped out and moved the crowd back. Their ladder was much longer, and soon a big, strong, fire-dinosaur was coming down it with Dilly firmly under one arm.

Everyone cheered. And it didn't take Dilly long to perk up, either. The moment his feet touched the ground, he asked if he could sit in the fire engine. And I could tell he thought the fire-dinosaur who had saved him was pretty wonderful . . .

"Now promise me you won't do anything that silly ever again, Dilly," said Mother when we were on our way home. "I don't think my nerves will stand it."

"I promise, Mother," said Dilly. "Besides, my next rescue will be *much* better. I've decided I'm going to be a fire-dinosaur. Can you make me a new costume?"

"If you do, Mother," I said before she had a chance to reply, "just don't let him wear it outside the house!"

"Don't worry, Dorla," said Mother with a smile. "I think I've learned my lesson!"

DILLY AND THE BIKE

It was my birthday a couple of weeks ago, and I had a really great time. Five of my friends came with me to MacDinosaurs for a party, and I got lots of presents.

The best one was from Mother and Father. It's a brand new bike, and it's beautiful. It's bright blue, it has five gears, and a special tail carrier at the back.

Of course, the only problem was my

pain of a little brother. He was very jealous, and he pestered me for a ride on my bike all day. He's been doing the same ever since.

He's tried everything he can to make me say yes. He's begged and pleaded, and he's even offered to give me some of his pocket money. I just keep saying no.

But that's a word Dilly doesn't understand. So I've been trying to sneak out on my bike without him noticing – although it doesn't always work.

Take the other Saturday, for instance. In the middle of the morning we had a drink and a snack, then Dilly sat down to watch TV. Usually you can't shift him once the cartoons are on.

Now's my chance, I thought. I asked Father if I could go out, and he said I could. But I hadn't got any further than the front gate when Dilly appeared at the door.

"Where are you going, Dorla?" he said. "Can I come? Will you let me have a ride on your bike?"

"You must be joking," I said. "I wouldn't let you touch my bike if you were the last dinosaur on Earth."

"*Please*, Dorla," said Dilly in his whiny,

begging voice. "I'll . . . I'll let you play with my magic eggshell."

"Big deal," I said. "I outgrew things like that long before I was your age. They're only for *babies*."

"I am *not* a baby!" shouted Dilly, and stamped his foot.

"Oh yes you are," I said. "Only babies stamp their feet."

"You're horrible, Dorla," said Dilly. "And I *hate* you!"

Then he opened his mouth, and . . . that's right, you guessed it, he let rip with an ultra-special, 150-mile-per-hour super-scream, the kind that makes me clap my paws over my ears and keep my eyes shut so tight I don't see Father come running out.

"All right, all right," he said, once Dilly stopped screaming. "What's the argument about this time?" We both

17

started to speak at once, but Father held his paw up. "Don't tell me. It's about Dorla's bike, isn't it?"

"I just wanted a go," said Dilly. "But *she* never lets me."

"You shouldn't *expect* Dorla to let you have a ride, Dilly," said Father. I turned to Dilly and gave him a So-There look. "But you *could* also occasionally try being nice to your little brother, Dorla."

Now Dilly stuck his tongue out at me, and soon we were yelling at each other again.

"QUIET!" shouted Father at the top of his voice. "That's it, I give up. You're both as bad as each other. So you can both go indoors and stay in your rooms until supper. Maybe that way I'll get some peace and quiet."

I went up to my bedroom, and sat on my bed feeling miserable. Then I remembered I had something that might help make me feel more cheerful – my secret store of sugar cane.

Now I've got a bike, I can go down to the shop at the end of our street and buy things without Mother and Father knowing. They don't want us to eat too much sugar cane. They say it's bad for our teeth. I know they're right but I only buy a little. And I do love it.

I keep it in a special hiding place I made behind some books on one of my shelves. I took a piece out and began sucking. It was delicious.

Suddenly I heard footsteps on the landing, and I realised my bedroom door wasn't shut. I put the sugar cane back, and dashed over to the bed. I picked up the first comic I could find, and pretended to read. But nobody came in.

"What are you doing, Dilly?" I heard Father saying. "I thought I told you to stay in your room."

"I was only going to the bathroom, Father," said Dilly.

"Well hurry up, will you?" said Father. "I might need to use it myself some time this week."

"Yes, Father," said Dilly in his I'm-Being-Such-A-Good-Little-Dinosaur voice.

I heard the bathroom door shut, then Father going into his bedroom. I breathed out slowly and smiled to myself.

Eventually, Father told us that if we said we were sorry, we could come out of our rooms. We both said we were, and a little later I asked if I could go out on my bike.

"I don't see why not," said Father. "So long as you take Dilly with you. After all, you *are* going to be the best of friends from now on . . . isn't that right?"

"OK, Father," I said. Just by looking at his face, I knew I had no choice. "You win."

Father called Dilly. For some reason, it took ages for him to come downstairs.

When he did, he looked oddly pleased with himself. He skipped happily up the street, and I followed gloomily behind on my bike.

We were going to Fern Hill, a place where there are some bike tracks and an adventure playground. It's just behind our house, so we don't have to go near any traffic.

As soon as we arrived, Dilly turned and stood in front of me.

"You're going to let me have a go on your bike now, aren't you, Dorla?" he said. He seemed pretty sure of himself.

"Don't start that again, Dilly," I said.

"But you have to," he said, smugly. "Your door was open and I saw what you did. You've got a secret store of sugar cane."

My heart sank. So Dilly hadn't been going to the bathroom earlier. He had been spying on *me*. And now he said he'd tell Mother and Father about the sugar cane – unless I let him have a go on my bike.

I was trapped. I didn't want to give in to him. But I didn't want Mother and Father to find out what I'd been up to, either.

So for the next half hour I pushed Dilly up and down Fern Hill. It turned out his legs were too short to reach the pedals on my bike. But it didn't matter while he had me as his slave. I think he enjoyed *that* even more than riding my bike.

"Come on, Dorla," he kept saying. "Push *harder*. I want to go really fast."

I'd been getting angrier and angrier, and when he said it for the seventh or eighth time, I finally lost my temper. I didn't care any more if Mother or

Father found out. I just wanted to get back at him. So I did something I should never have done.

"OK, Dilly," I said when we were at the top of the hill. "You want to go fast? Well, here's where you get your wish."

Then I simply let him go.

At first he was smiling. But the smile vanished as the bike picked up speed down the slope. He began to wail, though he didn't wail for long. The front wheel must have hit something, for Dilly suddenly flew over the handlebars.

He landed with a CRASH! in a bush, and fell to the ground.

I was in fits of laughter. Not only had I got my revenge, it had been the funniest thing I'd ever seen.

But then I realised Dilly wasn't moving, and I started to worry. Oh, no,

I thought – what if he was hurt badly?

What if he was *dead*?

When I got to him, his eyes were shut, and he didn't seem to be breathing. Then suddenly his eyes opened, and he spoke.

"Made you look, made you stare, made you lose your underwear!" he said, and laughed. "Fooled you!"

I was so relieved he was all right, I laughed too.

Afterwards, Dilly *did* admit that he'd

been very scared. He said he never, ever wanted to ride my bike again. So at least I knew he wouldn't be pestering me any more.

And when we left the adventure playground, he also said he wouldn't tell Father what I'd done. I said that was nice, and promised to give him a piece of my sugar cane in return.

"I don't think you will," he said, and n off, giggling.

"Why's that, Dilly?" I said.

"I ate it all before we came out," he shouted back.

To be honest, it didn't really matter. But I still chased him on my bike all the way home.

I can't let him get away with *everything*, now – can I?

DILLY AND THE BIG KIDS

"Father, is it OK if I play in the front garden?" said Dilly.

"Sure, Dilly," said Father, who was getting supper ready. "Just don't trample on my swamp roses."

Dilly said he wouldn't, and scampered out. I saw his tail was all curled up and quivering, and that usually means he's excited. So I knew he had more on his mind than some new game.

I was right, too. I kept an eye on him

27

from a window, and at first he acted very strangely. He wasn't doing any playing. He just stood there looking up the street.

Then I heard a lot of yelling and shouting. Three young dinosaurs came tearing down the pavement on skateboards. Dilly ran out to meet them with a smile on his face.

I knew who they were, of course. Their names are Donnie, Delbert and Davy, and they're in my year at school. And now I also knew what Dilly was up to.

For some reason he thinks they're really fantastic. I can't understand it, but he's *desperate* to make friends with them. Of course, they're not interested in *him* at all.

"Hello!" said Dilly eagerly. "I've been waiting for you . . . Would you like to play with me?"

"No *way*, man," said Donnie, swerving and just missing him. "Come on, guys. Last one on the ramp is a dingbat!"

The three of them flew off, leaving Dilly far behind. He turned round and trailed back indoors, his tail straight and limp. He looked so pathetic I *almost* felt sorry for him.

Dilly was unusually quiet at supper. At most mealtimes, no one else can get a word in edgeways. But that evening, he hardly said a word.

Mother and Father didn't notice, though. They were too busy talking about some dinosaurs we knew who had moved to another area. We had got a letter from them that morning.

"It's taking them ages to settle in," Mother said. "They hardly know a soul yet, and they've been there six months!"

"Making friends can be very hard, especially if you're an outsider," said Father. "They ought to throw a party."

"Is that a good way to make friends, Father?" said Dilly, looking up.

"There's none better, Dilly," said Father.

"Well, can *I* have a party . . . tomorrow?" said Dilly.

"Certainly not," said Mother very

quickly. "I still haven't got over the *last* party you had."

Neither had I. Dilly's birthday party had been a complete disaster. He had invited all the little dinosaurs from his nursery school, and they had nearly wrecked the house. It took us a week to calm him down afterwards, as well.

Mother and Father asked Dilly why he was keen to have a party. He wouldn't say, so I told them he wanted to be friends with Donnie, Delbert and Davy. Dilly gave me a mean look.

"Ah, I see," said Father in the voice he always uses when he's trying to explain something Dilly won't like. "They're probably a bit too old for you to play with anyway, Dilly . . ."

Dilly tried to make them change their minds, but Mother and Father wouldn't give in. There was definitely *not* going to be a party, and that made Dilly very sulky indeed.

But worse was to come for him. Mother and Father said they had something important to announce. They were going away for the weekend – *without* Dilly and me.

Mother explained we wouldn't be on our own. Grandma and Grandpa were coming to look after us, which I thought was fine. But Dilly absolutely *hates* being left out of anything, so I was sure he would make a fuss, and of course he did.

"I don't want to stay here with Grandma and Grandpa," he said. "I want to go with *you*. Grandma does nothing but make yucky cakes, and Grandpa spends all his time working in the garden. They're so *boring*!"

"You know that's not true, Dilly," said Mother. She and Father were beginning to look a little anxious. "It will be lots of fun, just wait and see. Now, how about some swamp worms and ice cream? It's pineapple flavour, your favourite."

Dilly didn't say anything. Instead, he narrowed his eyes, opened his mouth and . . . that's right, you guessed it, he fired off an ultra-special, 150-mile-per-hour super-scream, the kind that breaks every plate, bowl and glass on the dinner table.

"I don't think Dilly wants any dessert, Mother," I said.

Mother said that wasn't very funny, and packed Dilly off to his room.

Dilly's bad mood lasted for the next couple of days. In fact, he was *so* grumpy, he wouldn't even say hello when Grandma and Grandpa arrived. He stayed in his room with the door shut.

Mother and Father were very worried,

and wondered if they ought to stay at home. But Grandma wouldn't hear of it.

"You go and enjoy yourselves," she said. "It will do you the world of good. We can handle Dilly, can't we, Grandpa?"

"No problem, dear," said Grandpa. "Now, I'll just pop outside and take a look at those swamp roses . . ."

Mother and Father went in the end. Grandma, Grandpa and I waved goodbye as they drove off. Dilly didn't. Mother and Father even had to go up to his room to give him a kiss.

Dilly's behaviour didn't improve much, although Grandpa did persuade him to come out to the front garden. He said he wanted Dilly to help him do some digging. He had already got me planting bulbs.

"You can make a start here, Dilly," said

Grandpa, handing him a small spade.
Dilly was still looking sulky. "I'll be out on
the pavement . . . this hedge needs a
good trimming."

A while later I heard some yelling and
shouting. I turned . . . and saw Donnie,
Delbert and Davy tearing down the
street on their skateboards. And
Grandpa was right in the way!

"Look out!" I shouted.

But it was too late. Donnie crashed
smack into Grandpa, then Delbert and

Davy piled into *them*. They all fell over in a tangle of arms, legs, tails, skateboards and gardening tools.

Grandma came running out of the house.

"Are you all right, dear?" she said to Grandpa.

"Oof, just about!" he said, rubbing the back of his leg. "It's a good job I'm a tough old dinosaur!"

Grandma and I helped him to his feet and brushed him down. He had a few bumps and bruises – but it was Donnie, Delbert and Davy who had come off second best. They all had nasty grazes on their knees and elbows.

Grandma insisted they go in with her to be cleaned up and have plasters put on their injuries. They didn't argue, and Grandma soon had them sorted out.

Donnie apologised for the accident,

and Grandpa told him not to worry.
Then Grandma asked if everyone would
like some cakes.

"It's lucky this happened when it did,"
she said. "I was just getting the first batch
out of the oven . . ."

All this time Dilly had been standing
there with a stupid look on his face.
I don't think he could believe that

Donnie, Delbert and Davy were actually in *his* house.

But they were, and they seemed to be enjoying themselves. They kept asking for more of Grandma's cakes, and they even laughed at Grandpa's dreadful jokes and stories.

"Ooh," said Dilly happily as he handed round another plate of cakes. "This is just like having a party, isn't it?"

Donnie, Delbert and Davy stayed for quite a while, and we got to know each other very well. I decided they weren't so bad. For boy dinosaurs, that is.

Donnie even let Dilly have a go on his skateboard.

And when it was time for them to leave, they asked if they could come back again the next day. Grandma said they would be more than welcome.

"Hey, Dilly," said Donnie as he got on

his skateboard. "Your Grandma and Grandpa are really cool. See you tomorrow!"

"Yeah, man," said Dilly, smiling. "You bet!"

As he walked back indoors, I could see his tail was all curled up and quivering with excitement . . .

When Mother and Father came home, they said they had enjoyed their weekend, although they had been worried about Dilly. They were *very* pleased to hear he hadn't misbehaved.

"Well, Dilly," said Father. "Did you miss us?"

"Sort of," said Dilly looking at his feet. Then he smiled. "But I wouldn't really mind if you go away again soon. How about next weekend?"

We all laughed, especially Grandma and Grandpa!

DILLY AND THE WEDDING

One day a couple of months ago we had some really exciting news. Uncle Dan and his girlfriend Darlene came to tell us they were getting married!

Dan is Father's younger brother, and he's always been our favourite uncle. We like Darlene, too, so we were delighted. But there was some even better news for *me*.

Darlene wanted me to be one of her bridesmaids!

Of course, I said yes straightaway. I was absolutely thrilled. Darlene had asked a couple of her nieces to be bridesmaids too, and we would all have lovely dresses to wear.

I felt a bit less thrilled when I heard what came next, though. Uncle Dan and Darlene asked Dilly if he would like to be a page at their wedding. Dilly looked confused.

Mother explained that girl dinosaurs who helped at weddings were called bridesmaids, but boy dinosaurs who did the same thing were called pages.

Dilly put on his I'm-Thinking-Very-Hard-About-This look.

"If bridesmaids and pages are the same," he said at last, in a very suspicious voice, "does that mean I'll have to wear a dress, like Dorla?"

"Don't worry, Dilly," said Mother,

laughing. "You'll have a nice outfit to wear, but it *definitely* won't be a dress."

"That's OK then," said Dilly with a big smile. "I'll do it. Can I go and play now?"

"Yes, Dilly," said Mother. "Just don't get as dirty as you did yesterday."

But Dilly wasn't listening. He had already run out into the garden. We could hear him making loud shooting noises. Like most of his horrible little friends, he loves playing nasty war games. Mother says it's a phase he'll grow out of.

"You might as well ask the sun not to shine as ask him not to get dirty," laughed Father. He turned to Uncle Dan and Darlene. "No matter where we go, Dilly finds some mud to fall in."

"That's right," said Mother. "It's the bane of my life. But have you noticed how he manages to keep that dratted

baseball cap of his clean even when the
rest of him is filthy?"

"Ah, that's because he knows we won't
let him wear it in bed otherwise," said
Father. "You can say what you like
about our son, dear, but you couldn't
ever call him stupid."

I could. Well, how would you describe
someone who insists on wearing a dumb
baseball cap the whole time, even when
he's having a bath or he's in bed? And
all because it says 'Dinosaur Warrior' on
the front, over a picture of a big gun!

Mother and Father can't even
remember where they got it. Dilly
simply appeared at breakfast one
morning with it on. He claimed he'd
found it in his toy cupboard. Mother
said where Dilly's toy cupboard was
concerned, anything was possible.

Uncle Dan and Darlene stayed to tea,

and before they left, Mother arranged to meet Darlene at the Shopping Cavern with Dilly and me the next week. I could hardly wait – for that's when I was going to see my bridesmaid's dress!

Darlene was outside the shop with her two nieces when we arrived. We went in, and a nice lady dinosaur showed us catalogues with pictures of dresses in them. Darlene chose a style, and then we started trying things on.

Dilly, meanwhile, was being a real pest. He crawled around on the floor making those dreadful shooting noises. In the end, Mother had to tell him to stop and behave himself. So then he just sat in a corner looking bored and sulky.

The only time he laughed was when I came out of the changing room wearing a dress that was bright yellow.

"Ugh! What a *yucky* colour!" he said,

smirking. "I think I'm going to throw up."

Dilly sat holding his stomach and pretending to be sick. But I didn't care. I knew something *he* didn't.

"You think you're so clever, don't you?" I said. "Well, just wait till you see what they've got lined up for *you*, buster."

Dilly looked puzzled. He had forgotten he was there to be measured for an outfit as well. And judging from the styles Mother and Darlene had been looking at, I had a feeling he wasn't going to be very happy . . .

Usually, Dilly wears T-shirts and Bermuda shorts, or baggy dungarees with big pockets where he can keep all the vile things he picks up.

But when *he* came out of the changing room, he was wearing proper trousers, a white shirt with a bow tie, a velvet jacket, and shiny black shoes. He looked as though steam was about to come out of his ears.

"Why, Dilly, I wouldn't have thought you could be so smart," said Mother. I spluttered, and Mother nudged me in the back. "Tell your brother his outfit is terrific, Dorla," she hissed out of the corner of her mouth.

"Er . . . you look great, Dilly," I said, and bit my lip.

"No I *don't*," shouted Dilly. Then he

stamped his foot. "I look silly, and I *won't* wear these clothes to the wedding!"

Mother took a deep breath, the way

she always does when she's trying to be patient with Dilly, then told him he would have to. Dilly wanted to know why he couldn't wear his ordinary clothes. Mother said they weren't suitable.

"What, not even my Dinosaur Warrior cap?" he said.

"*Especially* not your Dinosaur Warrior baseball cap," said Mother. "And that's the end of it."

But it wasn't. Dilly opened his mouth and . . . that's right, you guessed it, he stunned us all with an ultra-special, 150-mile-per-hour super-scream, the kind that makes Mother really embarrassed, and guarantees him a good telling-off.

Over the next few days Dilly was very stubborn, and simply refused to give in. He kept saying he wouldn't wear his new outfit, and Mother and Father got more and more worried. In the end they said that, just this once, they'd buy him a present if he did.

Of course, Dilly changed his mind *instantly*.

At first I was disgusted. They'd never done anything like that for *me*. But then they said I could have a present too, so that was all right. Besides, I didn't want to be shown up at the wedding by my little brother any more than they did.

If only I'd known . . .

At last the big day came. There was some rain in the morning, but the sky had cleared by the time we got to the church. It was wonderful to see all our relatives, and meet Darlene's family. Uncle Dan looked handsome, but *very* nervous.

We stood in the churchyard while we waited for Darlene. Everyone told me how nice I looked, and Mother and Father got talking to some cousins we hadn't seen for ages. Then suddenly a look of slight panic passed across Mother's face.

"Does anyone know where Dilly is? I haven't seen him since we arrived . . ."

I knew what Mother was thinking. When Dilly goes missing, it usually means that he's up to some mischief.

He was, too. We found him in the corner of the churchyard playing a war game with two little dinosaurs from Darlene's family. He had been crawling around on the ground, and he was covered in mud from head to foot.

"Er . . . sorry, Mother," said Dilly with his biggest I-Know-I've-Done-Wrong-But-Please-Don't-Tell-Me-Off look on his face. "Come and see what we've been doing. I'm winning! I didn't know weddings would be such fun."

I thought Mother was bound to explode, but she never got the chance. Just at that moment Darlene's car pulled up outside the church, and we all had to hurry in.

Which explains why Darlene's page left a trail of muddy footprints as he walked up the aisle behind her. And that's not all he did, either. Just as the

vicar started speaking, Dilly produced his Dinosaur Warrior cap from a pocket and put it on.

I looked at Mother and Father. Mother was shaking her head, and Father had a paw over his eyes.

And like everyone else in the church, including the vicar, they were both trying very, very hard not to laugh.

In the end, so many good things happened that nothing could have spoiled the day. The service was lovely, and we had a marvellous party afterwards.

Mother and Father did give Dilly a telling-off, although they weren't too hard on him, mostly because he promised he would never, ever be naughty again.

But somehow I think we've heard that before – haven't we?

DILLY DINOSAUR, SUPERSTAR

Rex and the Rockosaurs are signing copies of their new record at the Shopping Cavern. But it's so crowded, Dilly can't get near them. So he lets out one of his ultra-special, 150-mile-per-hour super-screams — and Superstar Rex can hardly believe his ears!

DILLY GOES TO SCHOOL

In this fourth book about the adventures of Dilly, the dinosaur with the 150-miles-per-hour super-scream, Dilly goes to school for the very first time – and enjoys it so much he even wants to go at the weekend! Dilly also watches a horror film, meets Deevoo the baby dinosaur and organises his very own picnic . . .

DILLY THE ANGEL

"I'M GOING TO BE . . . AN ANGEL!" shouted Dilly.

When Dilly gets a part as an angel in his school's Christmas play, he isn't very pleased — but in the end his 150-mile-per-hour super-scream saves the show.

In this ninth collection of stories, Dilly also does some mending, goes to the funfair and tries to catch a burglar . . .

DILLY GOES ON HOLIDAY

Dilly and his family are off on holiday to the Swamp Land theme park. Dilly is sure he's going to have fun — but isn't too pleased when he finds that he's going to have to join the Tiny Tails. Then Dilly meets Dee who looks after the Tiny Tails — and decides that he's going to have a good holiday after all!

In this tenth book about Dilly the Dinosaur, Dilly also takes part in a Sports Day, puts on a magic show and finds a pet.

A Selected List of Fiction from Mammoth

While every effort is made to keep prices low, it is sometimes necessary to increase prices at short notice. Mandarin Paperbacks reserves the right to show new retail prices on covers which may differ from those previously advertised in the text or elsewhere.

The prices shown below were correct at the time of going to press.

☐	7497 1421 2	**Betsey Biggalow is Here!**	Malorie Blackman	£2.99
☐	7497 0366 0	**Dilly the Dinosaur**	Tony Bradman	£2.99
☐	7497 0137 4	**Flat Stanley**	Jeff Brown	£2.99
☐	7497 0568 X	**Dorrie and the Goblin**	Patricia Coombs	£2.50
☐	7497 0983 9	**The Real Tilly Beany**	Annie Dalton	£2.99
☐	7497 0592 2	**The Peacock Garden**	Anita Desai	£2.99
☐	7497 0054 8	**My Naughty Little Sister**	Dorothy Edwards	£2.99
☐	7497 0723 2	**The Little Prince (colour ed.)**	A. Saint-Exupery	£3.99
☐	7497 0305 9	**Bill's New Frock**	Anne Fine	£2.99
☐	7497 1530 8	**Who's a Clever Girl, Then?**	Rose Impey	£2.99
☐	7497 0041 6	**The Quiet Pirate**	Andrew Matthews	£2.99
☐	7497 0420 9	**I Don't Want To!**	Bel Mooney	£2.99
☐	7497 1496 4	**Miss Bianca in the Orient**	Margery Sharp	£2.99
☐	7497 0048 3	**Friends and Brothers**	Dick King Smith	£2.99
☐	7497 0795 X	**Owl Who Was Afraid of the Dark**	Jill Tomlinson	£2.99
☐	7497 0915 4	**Little Red Fox Stories**	Alison Uttley	£2.99

All these books are available at your bookshop or newsagent, or can be ordered direct from the address below. Just tick the titles you want and fill in the form below.

Cash Sales Department, PO Box 5, Rushden, Northants NN10 6YX.
Fax: 01933 414047 : Phone: 01933 414000.

Please send cheque, payable to 'Reed Book Services Ltd.', or postal order for purchase price quoted and allow the following for postage and packing:

£1.00 for the first book, 50p for the second; **FREE POSTAGE AND PACKING FOR THREE BOOKS OR MORE PER ORDER.**

NAME (Block letters) ....

ADDRESS ....

....

☐ I enclose my remittance for ....

☐ I wish to pay by Access/Visa Card Number

Expiry Date

Signature ....

Please quote our reference: MAND